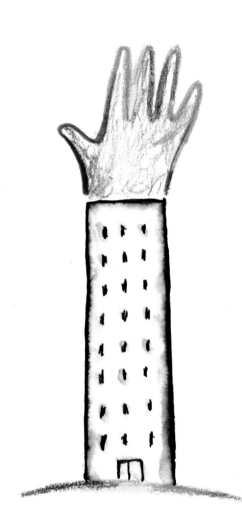

City Kids

street & skyscraper rhymes

X. J. Kennedy

City Kids

street & skyscraper rhymes

illustrations by

Philippe Béha

Vancouver
London

Contents

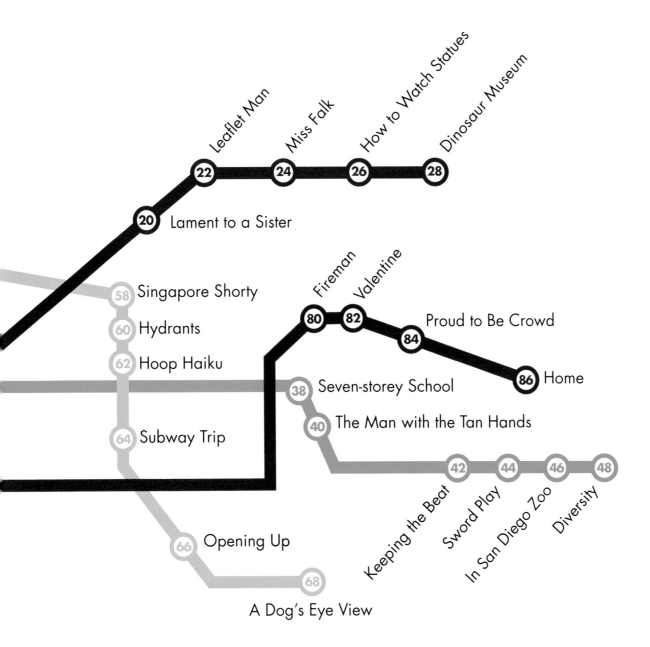

Leaflet Man
Miss Falk
How to Watch Statues
Dinosaur Museum

22 — 24 — 26 — 28

20 Lament to a Sister

Fireman
Valentine

58 Singapore Shorty

80 — 82

Proud to Be Crowd

60 Hydrants

84

62 Hoop Haiku

86 Home

38 Seven-storey School

40 The Man with the Tan Hands

64 Subway Trip

42 — 44 — 46 — 48

66 Opening Up

Keeping the Beat
Sword Play
In San Diego Zoo
Diversity

68

A Dog's Eye View

"For Dorothy, a city kid, as always." —X.J. Kennedy

ACKNOWLEDGEMENTS

Several of these poems first appeared in *SpinDrifter*, in the *Bulletin of the Nick Virgilio Haiku Association*, and in the anthologies *Carnival of the Animals*, edited by Gerard Benson, Judith Chernaik, and Cicely Herbert (Walker Books) and *Christmas Poems*, edited by Myra Cohn Livingston (Holiday House). In different versions, these first appeared in earlier collections: "The Man with the Tan Hands" in *Nude Descending a Staircase* (Doubleday); "How To Watch Statues," "Crash!," "Roofscape," "Valentine," "Where Will We Run To," and "Subway Trip" in *The Forgetful Wishing-well*; and "Walking the Sky" (formerly titled "Braves") in *The Kite That Braved Old Orchard Beach* (both Margaret K. McElderry Books).

soggy morning

My favourite treat's
   right after rain
when every street's
   a puddle chain.
In every pool
   I fling some rocks,
then sit in school
   with real cool socks.

who needs cow moos?

Who needs cow moos
and bleating sheep?
Give me a taxi
with a wicked BEEP!

Who needs tractors
and open spaces?
Give me a cable car
going places!

waiting to grow up

Tyrone, my brother who's real big,
Has a bright red motor bike.
He used to take me out on rides,
But now Petunia Pike
Clamps both arms tight around his waist
As they zoom off down the street.

I'll grow up. I can hardly wait.
Old age looks pretty neat.

deli restaurant

My Uncle Moe's a freak for food.
He says, "Must mind your belly,"
And making sure I'm minding mine,
He takes me to the deli.

There's not one seat that isn't full,
The soda's cold and fizzy.
Each table's got a mustard pot
And every pot keeps busy.

We order bagels pink with lox,
Dill pickles, hard salami,
A paste of chicken livers on
Thick black bread, hot pastrami.

When aproned Becky pats his head
And says, "How 'bout it, honey,
Another cheesecake, cherries on?"
Says Unc, "Sure! I got money."

In Windsor's Landsbury Park

Playing hockey,
Feeling cocky,
   Whizzing down the ice!

Swing my stick
Double quick,
   Sink a goal in twice!

More sticks whack!
Fresh attack!
   But I'm slightly slow

To duck the puck—
What bad luck!
   Where'd my front teeth go?

Lament to a Sister

I'm always next
to use the phone
when you just ate
an ice cream cone.

I pick up the phone,
my fingers stick.
Why do you have
to talk and lick?

Leaflet Man

Right in the middle of the crowd
He stands and gives away
Leaflets to every passing hand.
I take one. What's it say?

Maybe, Try Brenda's Hair Salon
Or, Juicy steak at Nate's!—
Sometimes, Repent! The world will end!
Or, Lose weight fast! Lift weights!

The man stays standing with his stack,
Just giving. Round him weaves
The crowd till he's left like a tree
Done shedding all its leaves.

miss falk

The oldest teacher in our school
  Is Miss Rosetta Falk.
She's grimmer than a graveyard ghoul,
  Her head-hair's white as chalk.

Her glasses' glass is ice-cube thick,
  It works just like a mirror
To let her look behind her back
  And see us all the clearer.

I'd like to tell a crocodile,
  Go get Miss Falk and feed!
But maybe I'll just wait a while
  Till she learns me how to read.

how to watch statues

Don't snicker and sneer
And say, *What is it?*
Just open your eyes
And let it visit.

Stationed in stone,
This discus-thrower
Has thrown a long time
And grown no slower.

Here's a statue that's only
Rectangles of red.
Think you could do better?
So go ahead.

Here's a strange baboon
That will take you far.
For its skull Picasso
Used an old toy car.

All you do is stand
In front of a statue
Till, ready to talk,
It looks right at you.

dinosaur museum

Old monster lizards stiffly stand,
All totally undressed:
They don't have eyeballs, flesh or skin.
They laid eggs in a nest.

Once long ago a passing comet
~~...~~ "...~~...~~ why don't I bomb it?"
~~...~~ rds
~~...~~ rds.

~~...~~
~~...~~ und
~~...~~ le
The way you do a jigsaw puzzle.

aQuariUm

Flashes of fishes, quick flicks of tails.
Scoot scurry scamper of scattering scales.
A sponge blows bubbles, sea horses race,
Anemones wave tentacles of slow pink lace.

A whale of a sailfish unfolds a fin,
Fans a whiskery walrus with a double chin.
A shovelhead shark grins, his mouth underneath
Like a cave full of stalactites—steel-knife teeth.

The ocean brims over with creatures, it seems,
That swim past my eyes like remembered dreams.
From behind glass, a couple of curious squid
Stare out at me: *Hey, where's your fishfins, kid?*

crash!

Truck stopped.
Taxi didn't.
Bumpers bopped.
Windshield splintered.

"You dumb klutz!" says Truck,
"Why didn't you stop?"
"I did," says Hack.
Fists whack.

neighbours

Old Mrs. Creedle
Can't thread her own needle.
Her hands shake. Down the hall
She yelps for help. I always run
When that old lady calls.

She's good to me.
She stitches my rips
And once she made a toy
Brown bear with two Lifesaver eyes
For my little sister Joy.

One day when Poppa heard her fall
Ka-thump, he ran and found
Her lying stone cold on the floor.
Those bruises don't show anymore.
Us neighbours, we're around.

tires

When Poppa comes to Momma's place
To visit me, he hires
A boy to keep watch on his car
So no one takes the tires

Because last time he came he lost
All four, but Poppa say,
"Why, girl, it's worth a heap of tires
To see you, any day."

Seven-Storey School

in London NW2

Each morning when I scrub my teeth
And face, so does the sun,
And by the time I've bussed to school
My homework sums are done.

Our school is seven storeys high,
I'm glad it hasn't more.
We study gas in science class
While outside, lorries roar.

Sometimes your head turns powder-white
From flakes of snowing plaster.
"Just brush your hair," Doc Morton says.
(He's who we call Headmaster.)

Our football field's a mile away
And in the room we lunch in
You're jammed up close to someone else—
Is it his lunch you're munchin'?

But ours is said to be a school
You're glad you went to, later,
So up and down all day we crawl
In a mud-turtle elevator.

the man
with the tan hands

The man
with the tan
hands
who stands
and scoops up
roast
chest-
nuts
in cups
of old
news
folded
like perching
birds
sold
me a few
new
words.

keeping the Beat

San Francisco street performer's rap

Who needs to sleep?
Why take time to eat?
All I want to do
is keep the beat!
Want to race like a spaceship,
decompress,
want to rocket uptown
like the Pony Express,
want to be a mosquito,
want to flit and fly,
cut a slice of sidewalk
like a piece of pie,
want to do a handstand,
run round on my knees,
want to buzz you, honey,
like a bunch of bees,
want to keep on rolling
like a real steel wheel,
want to shock people like
an electric eel,
drive lazy toes crazy,
light a heat in your feet?
Any old way I
can keep that beat.

Sword Play

In all Quebec there's no better baker
Than Monsieur Beaupain. For a real tooth-breaker,

Just take a big bite of his good chewy bread!
Try a round rye boule the size of your head

Or a crusty baguette as long as a sword.
My buddy Michel and me don't get bored

When we bring home the bread, cause we're always fooling.
We fence with our loaves, make believe we're dueling,

And my folks don't know when they sit down to dinner
That my baguette was a two-time winner.

in san diego zoo

How patiently the elephant
Stands tall in his stall all day,
Occasionally flapping a delicate ear
To shoo a blue fly away.

He drops a big poo and a lady says, "Phew!
Why, the filthy beast!" I suppose
All he gets for his pay is the bundle of hay
That he hoists with his wonderful nose,

But perhaps he dreams of blossoms and streams
On a veldt where he once roamed free.
Me, I'd get in a rage at my narrow cage
If the elephant were me.

47

diversity

Folks say our school needs more diversity.
I guess that means
You wouldn't be happy to find in a bag
All the same-colour jellybeans.

graffiti

Someone last night with brush and paint
Drew wavy lines on the streetside wall
Of our building. He didn't know how to draw small.
He thinks he's an artist? Well, he sure ain't.

And yet when I kind of squinch up my eyes
His zigzaggy stuff, to my surprise,
Looks pretty. It's better, after all,
Than the cold blank stare of an empty wall.

haymarket square

To Haymarket on Saturday Mom and I go
Where red apples sit glimmering, row on row,
Pineapples poke out their thorny noses,
And people say "Ouch," grabbing pickery roses,
Where the peas need to please a demanding crowd
And pinching the peaches is not allowed.

It's late afternoon when we always shop,
When the watermelon takes a big price-drop
And a dollar buys six heads of romaine lettuce—
Why, they practically throw the tomatoes at us!
Then with eats for our family to last all week,
We lug home bags crammed so full they creak.

my aim in life

I wouldn't mind being a traffic cop,
Raise my magic-wand hand, make everything stop,
Clear the way for an ambulance, fire truck or hearse,
And whistle at a pickpocket pinching a purse.

in the library

I love to search on the main computer.
I'm a champion hacker, a real cool booter.

I look up a book I've long intended
To read—there's its number! My search is ended!

Like, wow! Like I found me a birthday present!
I run to the shelf—but there it isn't.

Well, that book left me in the lurch,
But—hooray! I can start me a whole new search!

Singapore Shorty

Singapore Shorty is a finding man.
He's good at rummaging a full trash can
For things to recycle, worth a nickel each.
He searches alleys, he combs the beach
For valuable bottles that he turns in.
He leaves the world cleaner where he has been.

Each night he goes home with his bulging bag,
So tired that his feet in their old shoes drag.
His house is a box tucked under a bridge
With a Styrofoam cooler for his kitchen fridge
And a crazy old lady who gives him kisses
And a one-eyed tomcat that spits and hisses.

hydrants

Like taxis at curbside
they're waiting for hire.
Does nobody need them
to put out a fire?

A hydrant-like doorman
in red, buttoned up,
regards with suspicion
an innocent pup.

On days when it heatwaves
us kids scamper out
in swimsuits. Then hydrants
unscrew, spurt and spout.

hoop haiku

Kid hoop star
slam-dunks in the parking lot
where thistles bloom through tar.

suBway trip

Roaring round a bend, train shrieks
Just like chalk on blackboards.
People talk, read books or stare.
Place-names pass like flashcards
While this train and I keep on
Flying uptown backwards.

Opening Up

On Saturday
I push a broom
For Mister Izzy Fine.
I sweep the doorstep,
Wind the clocks
And keep them all in line.
If one of them is running slow
I shove its hand ahead.
Old Mister Fine looks at the sky
And sighs and shakes his head:
"What weather! Life's not hard enough?"
He uncranks crease by crease
His slack-jawed awning—hear it scream
As if it gripes for grease.

a dog's eye view

For us city dogs, the breakneck pace
Of traffic makes it hard to chase
A cat across the street. It's hard
To hide bones in not much backyard,

But if your deli man is nice
When slicing meat, you get a slice,
And when it snows and streets grow wetter
You get to wear your knitted sweater.

Laundromat

When Mom goes to the laundromat
She takes me, cause I'm old
Enough to carry stacks of stuff
And I know how to fold.

We shell out quarters. Underwear
Swirls in a soapy waltz,
Socks leapfrog over other socks,
Pop's pants do somersaults.

We drag 'em out. The dryer drum
Starts overturning. See
My bathrobe rock-and-rolling round—
More action than TV!

And when we've hauled our clean clothes home
I dream beside a heap
Of warm fresh stuff and toast my face.
In no time, I'm asleep.

street performers

A poet strums a hard rock beat,
Makes raps up right there in Yonge Street,

A guy with hair like copper wire
Sips gasoline and spits out fire,

A juggler juggles dinner plates
While turning somersaults on skates,

Another show is hard to pass:
A man jumps barefoot on smashed glass.

But my favourite show is small and funky—
The organ grinder's dressed-up monkey.

roofscape

The sun in white whiskers
is striding the roof
ignoring the warning sign
DANGER! KEEP OFF!

From far below echo
the booms of dumped cans
and, windily whirring,
big air-cooling fans.

Tanks stuffed full of water
like dragonflies perch.
A skyscraper shadows
a low-kneeling church.

Walking in the Sky

My friend Mark, he's one special boy,
A real live fifth-grade Iroquois,
And once I saw in all the papers
About his dad, who builds skyscrapers.

Some architects ran out of luck.
Atop a half-built building, stuck,
They stood up there and hollered murder
Till Mark's dad coolly climbed a girder.

Against the sky, up where it's scary,
He walked as though he walked a prairie,
Unruffled as an eagle's wings,
And lowered them in fireman's slings.

When he grows up, Mark says, he dreams
He'll skywalk too and weld steel beams.

where will we run to

Where will we run to
when the moon's
polluted in its turn

and the sun sits
with its wheels blocked
in the used

             star

                 lot?

fireman

Anthony Farrell the fireman
Is gone. He'd let me climb
Into the driver's seat of the engine,
Pretend I was roaring to a fire.
I used to feed his white black-spotted dog
Leftover steak bones. He'd tell
Me stories of fires he'd helped put out,
Hearing flames crackle, people yell.

I think about how Anthony met
The worst fire ever, all
Those people running hollering down stairs
In the World Trade tower ready to fall,
And Anthony, holding his face to the fire,
Climbing to face it, higher, higher.

vaLentine

If all the whole world's taxicabs
Came running to my call,
I'd park right by your door and honk
In the shiniest cab of all.

We'd drive to Vancouver, Cairo, Rome—
Could anything be sweeter
Than ticking off a million miles
Upon a metal meter?

proud to be crowd

I stand in the crowd with my head unbowed
Though it's raining. Today's the day
When our Red Sox team has fulfilled our dream
And we owe them a huge HOORAY.

I'm proud to be crowd cheering long and loud,
Being part of a victory.
Oh, I may be only a shout in a crowd,
But I'll never stop being me.

home

East Side, West Side,
all around the town,
which side
is the best side?
Wherever you sit down
to eat your supper, pet your cat,
do homework, watch TV—
any old place
that's your home base
is where you want to be.

LIBRARY AND ARCHIVES CANADA
CATALOGUING IN PUBLICATION

Kennedy, X. J.
    City kids : street and skyscraper rhymes / X.J. Kennedy ;
illustrations by Philippe Béha.

Interest age level: For ages: 8-12.
ISBN 978-1-896580-44-9

    1. City children--Juvenile poetry. 2. Children's poetry,
American.
I. Béha, Philippe II. Title.

PS3521.E563C58 2009 j811'.54 C2009-904851-5

CATALOGUING AND PUBLICATION DATA AVAILABLE FROM THE BRITISH LIBRARY.

Book design by Elisa Gutiérrez
The book is set in Mrs. Eaves, Bighouse and Pickelpie for the title.

10 9 8 7 6 5 4 3 2 1

Printed and bound in China on ancient-forest-friendly paper.

Manufactured by Kings Time Canada
(Subsidiary of Nordica International Ltd.)
Manufactured in Panyu, Guangzhou, China
in November 2009.
Job # 11/69/09

The publisher wishes to thank the Government of Canada
and Canadian Heritage for their financial support through
the Canada Council for the Arts, the Book Publishing
Industry Development Program (BPIDP) and the Association
for the Export of Canadian Books (AECB). The publisher
also wishes to thank the Government of the Province of
British Columbia for the financial support it has extended
through the Book Publishing Tax Credit program and the
British Columbia Arts Council.

 Canada Council   Conseil des Arts
for the Arts   du Canada

 BRITISH
COLUMBIA
ARTS COUNCIL